# ALL CHAOS FOR THIEVES

## Scales Of Justice
### Book 0.5

## LAURA GREENWOOD

Visit Laura Greenwood's website at:

www.authorlauragreenwood.co.uk

Cover by Ravenborn Designs

All Chaos For Thieves is a work of fiction. Names, characters, places, and incidents are the products of the author's imagination or are used fictitiously. Any resemblance to actual persons, living or dead, businesses, companies, events, or locales is entirely coincidental.

If you find an error, you can report it via my website. Please note that my books are written in British English: https://books.authorlauragreenwood.co.uk/errorreport

To keep up to date with new releases, sales, and other updates, you can join my mailing list via my website or The Paranormal Council Reader Group on Facebook.

## Blurb

**Sometimes a bit of thievery is the only way to live.**

Rera does what she has to in order to survive, even when that means doing something that could damn her soul - robbing a tomb.

But nothing is as straightforward as it seems, and Rera's conflicting feelings only deepen the further she gets involved with the London underworld.

Can she escape the eyes of the goddess of justice who seems to be watching her everywhere she goes?

-

All Chaos For Thieves is a prequel to the Scales Of Justices series, an urban fantasy series based on Egyptian mythology and set in the same world as The Apprentice Of Anubis.

If you love Egyptian mythology, alternative versions of the modern day, temple politics, slow-burn workplace romance, and a world where the gods are real, then the Scales Of Justice series is for you!

## A Brief Note

The Egyptian Empire World is set in an alternative universe where the Egyptian Empire never fell and replaced the Roman Empire. The split in the timeline happened after the Ptolemaic dynasty and the final Cleopatra's infamous reign. Instead of Egypt falling into the hands of the Romans, they fought back and gained control of the budding Roman Empire. All religions still exist in the world, but many have been absorbed into the Egyptian religion (this was common practice during their ancient history, so is something I adopted into the series).

For the purposes of this series, the Egyptian Empire spans much of Africa and Europe, as well as some of the Middle East.

I made the decision to keep a lot of the words and systems we use today (including place names like London and the River Thames) to make the reading experience as smooth as possible. If this was the real progression of events, those things would likely have been named differently.

Things I have kept are the Ancient Egyptian concept of a week (10 days, including a 2 day "weekend"), month (3 weeks), season (4 months) and year (3 seasons plus 5 feast days). The currency they're using is debens (derived from the Ancient Egyptian word for bread - something workers were often paid in). Names have also been influenced by Ancient Egyptian history.

# Chapter 1

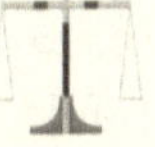

The alarm blares and I roll over, grabbing my phone to turn it off while I let out a tired groan. I hate getting up this early, but if I want to make sure my little sister gets off to school in time, I've got to do it. Especially because if I leave her to her own devices, I know she'll just skip a day. This is one of the many times I wish my parents were actually involved in our lives and not off doing their own thing.

I throw off the covers and grab my jumper, pulling it over my head and hoping it'll be enough to stave off the chill seeping in through the hole in the window that our landlord refuses to fix. He'll raise the rent easily enough, but actually taking care of the property so it's live-able is another matter.

I push the annoyance aside and head through to the small kitchen, banging on Meri's door as I pass. "Time to get up."

"I am!" she calls back, sounding surprisingly awake.

I open the fridge and grimace at the sight of precisely nothing. I haven't had time to go to the shops, and even if I had, it's not like I have a particularly big budget to work with. I let out a sigh and close it again, trying to think of what I'm going to make Meri to eat when there's nothing in the house. I'm barely five minutes into my day and I'm already failing at the most important job my dad left me to do.

As I'm thinking, the front door creaks open. The hinges need oiling, but at least it gives me a warning about anyone coming in. I reach for the first thing I can grab to defend myself and hold it out towards the intruder.

"Really, Rera? You're going to try and attack me with a spoon?" my best friend asks, running a hand through his unruly dark hair.

I roll my eyes at him and drop the spoon

back onto the side. "I could do some serious damage with a spoon."

"If anyone could, it would be you," Zet concedes. "But maybe don't."

"Mmm, wouldn't want to ruin your handsome face."

"Of course not. What would I impress the ladies with if you did?"

"You'd be left with your terrible sense of humour, and we can't have that," I throw back at him, knowing he's perfectly capable of taking it.

He clutches his hand to his chest. "You wound me. And to think I brought you breakfast." He sets a paper bag down on the table, the smell of freshly baked bread emanating from it.

My eyes widen. "What did you do?"

"I had a good morning," he responds cryptically.

I groan. "You stole it, didn't you?"

He shrugs. "We're thieves by trade," he points out. "What's it matter if I stole some breakfast?"

I don't have anything to say about that. Technically, I see his point. If we're going to get into trouble over what we do, it's not because he stole some bread this morning, it's probably going to be around the much more drastic kinds of theft we've been involved with. Particularly stealing from the temples, most of them frown down on that.

Before I can properly chastise Zet for his reckless choices, my sister comes out of her room, heading straight for the paper bag and pulling out a stuffed bread roll.

At least he stole the good stuff and didn't potentially damn his soul for stale bread.

"Are you ready for school?" I ask Meri.

She shoots me an unimpressed look. "Who's asking?"

"I am."

"You're not my mother."

"I know that, but Dad told me I had to look after you..."

"Until he gets back," she cuts me off. "Then he'll be in charge again."

It's all I can do to bite my tongue and not point out that Dad is never going to come back because he doesn't want to. All it will do is cause an argument, and right now, we have other things to focus on. It would be much easier if he'd actually made me Meri's guardian, at least then I'd have been able to tell her what to do with actual authority.

"Dad isn't here right now," I point out. "And if you want to gain employment as an apprentice in one of the temples..."

"Why would I want to serve the gods?" Meri asks, looking somewhat bored with the conversation already.

Zet chuckles and leans back against the counter, eating an apple. I'm not sure where he's got it. He probably stole it just like he did with the bread.

"Because it's a good living," I say to Meri, ignoring my best friend. I don't need to hear what he thinks of serving the gods, I'm well aware of his opinions. He's been making them clear to me for years.

"You don't serve the gods," my sister throws back at me with all of her young teenage bite. I should be glad that she has it, considering I'm barely five years older than her and have already had to do away with mine.

"I had to leave school so I can earn enough so we can keep living here," I remind her. "That's not what I want for you."

She scoffs, but continues eating. Hopefully,

that will mean there will be fewer arguments going forward. She finishes her food and heads back to her room, slamming the door shut behind her.

I let out a frustrated sigh.

"She's not wrong, you know," Zet says.

"About what?" I take one of the other stuffed breads from the bag. It's already stolen, I might as well eat it.

"Not wanting to serve the gods."

I sigh. "You think I want that? The temples are only there to run our lives. But the priests make good money, and we could always use some of that."

"We make good money."

I snort without meaning to. "Do we? Because I can barely keep up with rent, never mind everything Meri needs for school."

"You could ask your dad..."

"No," I shut him off as firmly as I dare to. Asking my dad is *not* something I'm even going to consider.

He shrugs and throws his apple core into the window box I'm attempting to grow some carrots in. It's not going very well, but I'm hoping that it'll happen eventually. "So which priesthood should she join, Rera?" he asks. "Sekhmet so she's a priestess hunting the streets for us? Or Ma'at so that she can punish us once we're caught? Maybe she'll even be one of the priestesses who claim they can tell when people are lying."

"You don't think they can?" I ask.

He shrugs. "I think people are scared of lying to them."

"Hmmm." I don't know what to think. Everyone knows that some of Ma'at's priests can tell when you're lying to them, and I see no reason to think it isn't real.

But then again, I'm so far removed from the magic of the gods that I have no real way of knowing if any of what the priests say to be true is.

I sigh. "It doesn't matter anyway. No one we know ever joins the priesthood."

"Elitism at its best," Zet agrees.

Meri emerges from her room with her bag over her shoulder. "All right, I'm going to school. Are you happy?" The expression on her face says that *she's* not happy, but I barely care about that right now. She's going to school and that's a win.

"Yes," I respond, folding my arms and hoping that I'm not revealing how relieved I am that there isn't more of a fight to be had over it. She probably hates school as much as I did, but I can't let her drop out unless she really has to.

She rolls her eyes and heads out of the door, thankfully without any more protests.

"Remind me never to have kids," I mutter.

"You'll probably be dead before that's a possibility anyway," Zet says.

"Cheery thought."

"Better than being locked away by the Temple of Ma'at."

"So true," I murmur.

"Speaking of, we've got a job tonight," he says.

I raise an eyebrow. "Speaking of being caught and locked away by Ma'at?"

"Nah, just speaking of reasons they could do that to us."

"You better not be tempting fate, or I'm going to have to ask for a new partner," I murmur.

He laughs. "You can't get better than me, Rera."

"Jury's out," I throw back. "But if we're out tonight, then I'm going to get more sleep."

"Mind if I hang out here today?" he asks.

"Knock yourself out. Has Jan got his girlfriend around again?"

"Yep, and she is not quiet. There's no way I'm going to get any rest with them there. Your sofa is much more appealing."

"I'll warn you that the fridge is empty."

"Why do you think I brought food with me? I know you're terrible at keeping it stocked," he teases.

"I'm not terrible at it, I just don't have enough money to fill it."

"We need to get you some better-paying work."

I roll my eyes at him. It's really not as simple as that, and he knows it. I suppose it wouldn't be too bad if I could take a roommate like he does, but I have to support Meri, and that drains the little money I've got quickly.

"If I could, then I would. Maybe this job later will be the gateway to it." I doubt it. This will probably just be like every other job we've ever pulled, but I can live in hope.

Though I suppose if I'm going to dream of

unlikely events, then it should be that I suddenly find myself in possession of enough debens that I never have to work another day in my life. But that's not going to happen either.

Zet makes himself comfortable on the sofa, leaving me to head back to my bedroom with every intention of ignoring the world for the next few hours.

# Chapter 2

The early evening sunshine illuminates the boarded-up building which is more than it seems from the outside. I check around to make sure no one is watching me and move one of the boards out of the way so I can climb in through the broken window.

I check myself over before going any further to make sure I'm not suddenly bleeding, having cut myself on the glass shards several times before. In theory, I know where to put my hands now, but there's always a chance something's changed. Thankfully, everything seems intact.

"Finally, you took your time," Zet says, spotting me from the doorway opposite.

"I had to make sure Meri got home from school safe."

"She just turned thirteen, not five," he responds. "She's more than capable."

"Maybe," I mumble.

"We got into so much trouble when we were thirteen," he muses.

"I remember, that's why I want to make sure she doesn't. I don't want her to go down a life of crime too." It's too late for me, but that doesn't mean I can't stop it from happening to her.

"Aww, but is it really so bad?"

*Yes.* I don't answer him out loud. Partly because I know he doesn't really understand my aversion to it, but also because I don't know who else could be listening and who they might be reporting to. If the wrong person hears that I'm not all in, then it could end up with me turned over to Ma'at's priests by someone I'm supposed to trust.

"What's the job?" I ask instead as we make our way through into the prep room.

"Some rich guy is being buried in a couple of days."

I stop in my tracks. "Tomb robbing?"

"Yeah. Something wrong with that?" The

way he asks the question makes it clear that he expects me to say there's nothing, even if that isn't actually the truth.

I shrug instead of voicing my feelings, something I find I've been doing more and more often with Zet. "I've just never done one before." And I can't say I'm thrilled at the prospect of changing that.

"Well, tonight is the time to learn," Zet responds without missing a beat. "I did one with Geo the other week."

I look over to where the red-headed thief is prepping his kit for tonight. "You coming with us too, Geo?"

He looks up and smiles at me. "Not tonight. Akar and I are hitting up the new Temple of Ra near the Thames. Their security is still lax, which means their treasury should be ripe for the pickings."

I nod, knowing better than to question whether it's a good idea to steal from the gods. All I've gotten any time I do that is derision from the others, none of whom seem to be particularly worried about the eternal wrath of beings who might not exist. I'm not so convinced. The priesthood maintains power for many reasons, but I don't think it would have managed to do so for five thousand years without at least some of what they're saying being true.

But I can understand why most of the people in my line of work don't like thinking about it. If the gods are real, then our souls are never going to get to Duat, and the paradise promised to us will be denied instead. And that's if we're even properly buried in the first place. Most of the priests of Anubis claim that it's an insult to send a criminal to the Hall of Judgement in the first place. And I certainly count as that.

"Rera? Are you listening?" Zet asks me.

"Huh, sorry, I was in a world of my own," I respond. "Tell me again?"

He rolls his eyes and heads over to start packing the tools we're going to need. "The rich guy didn't spring for extra security and has gone for one of the burial grounds not owned by the Temple of Anubis, so it should be pretty straightforward. In, out, then gone."

"Right. Isn't it going to be a problem that there's so much open space around the tomb?"

It'll make us easy to spot for any of the guards from Sekhmet's temple prowling the streets.

Zet shakes his head and spreads out a map of London on the table. I head over to join him, leaning over even though I have no idea where our target is.

"Here," he says, tapping on the Tower Hamlets burial ground.

One side is surrounded by trees, which would actually give us decent cover if we decide that we want to make our getaway in that direction. On the other side are rows of orderly family homes. Not bad either. The kids will probably already be asleep by the time we get to the burial grounds, and the parents won't be far behind.

"What's security like?" I ask.

"Uncertain beyond lax," Zet responds.

"One guard," Geo puts in, coming over to join us. "Akar and I were over in that neck of the woods a couple of months ago and hid in the burial grounds when some guard priests appeared. We were the ones who reported it to the boss as an easy target. He's just been waiting for the right burial to come along."

"Right." An uneasy feeling settles within me,

but I'm not entirely sure why. This is my job. I want to get another one, but no one will hire me until I turn eighteen next week, and even then it's going to be hard without any school transcripts to prove my education. And I need money now.

"We'll have a cart, so we'll do as many trips into the tomb as we can," Zet says. "Start with the valuable but portable stuff and move upwards."

"Aren't they going to notice that stuff is missing?" I ask. This feels like the kind of situation that's going to backfire on us.

"Probably," Zet responds. "The important thing is that they don't link it back to us when they realise it is. But that should be the easy bit, we haven't been caught yet."

A part of me wants to point out that that's exactly the kind of thing someone who is just about to get caught tomb robbing would say, but I know better than that. Zet has many good qualities, but his recklessness definitely counts towards his bad ones.

Footsteps sound and the three of us look up in time to see Akar enter the room. "I brought dinner," he says, holding up four tightly sealed wraps.

My stomach rumbles loudly, not having had anything since the stuffed bread Zet brought this morning.

"Thanks, Akar," I say, taking it from him. My mouth waters at the scent of grilled chicken from Akar's parents' grill. It's one of the advantages of being sent out on the same evening as him.

"Hey, no biggie. Mum always wants rid of last night's chicken, so she reheats it for us."

I'm too hungry to really care about the reasoning behind it and devour the wrap, feeling a little better for having properly eaten and grateful that he always thinks to feed the rest of us before we go out for an evening's thievery. I'm not sure if he knows that some of us are struggling with the basics of life, but it's appreciated all the same.

"It's a good thing you brought it, or Rera's stomach might get us caught," Zet jokes.

I roll my eyes. "That's literally never happened."

"I thought it was going to once," he responds. "That time when we were fourteen and trying to get out of that shop with some sunglasses."

"It was your sneeze that nearly got us caught, not my stomach," I counter. "And it doesn't matter because we got away with it." And have been doing ever since, whether that's a good thing or not is up for debate.

"Well, as much as it's fun to hang out in a depleted building, we've got to get going," Geo says. "Good luck. We'll see you at the handover in the morning." He picks up a black duffel bag and swings it over his shoulder, heading out of the room with Akar following behind him.

"I guess that's our cue to get going too," I say to Zet, mostly because I just want this to be over.

"Yep." He hands me one of the bags he's packed.

I take a deep breath, the nerves that always assail me at this point of a job springing to life. It would be easier if I actually enjoyed what we did, but as it is, I'm just going to have to settle for doing it well enough that we don't get caught.

# Chapter 3

The shadows of the burial site appear in front of us without a single light in place to make it clear what's going on inside. If there really is only one guard, then it's no surprise that Geo reported this place as a potential mark, it's going to be easy for us to get in and out undetected, even with a cart.

I know that should make me happy, especially because I need the money, but instead, it's just an uncomfortable reminder of how we're taking advantage of situations like this.

Zet gestures for us to come to a stop in front of an ornate gate. The tops of the pillars are carved to look like lotus blossoms even though they're not native to the British Isles, and protective images are chiselled into the columns. Some of them are specific to the dead, but others are just general protective spells.

A shiver runs down my spine. Either these have no magic in them and no ability to deter anyone, or we'll face dire consequences and pay with our souls.

Maybe that's why they don't work. Our souls are already damned by the actions we take, what's a curse outside a burial site going to do to us that's worse than that?

Zet is having none of my internal struggles and has pulled out a pair of bolt cutters. Without even pausing for long enough to check it over for potential curses, he snips through the padlock holding the chain around the gate in place.

I wince at the sound of breaking metal, but my best friend doesn't even notice.

He whistles once, and a kid of about eight appears.

"Keep watch for us, won't you?" he asks, giving her a couple of coins.

"I'll give the signal if I see anything," she replies, puffing up her chest as if she's been given an important duty instead of being made part of a crime.

Zet nods.

I watch in slight horror as she hurries off to a nearby tree and scales up it, taking her place as our lookout.

"She's a kid," I hiss at my best friend.

He shrugs. "She's nearly nine. How old were you when your dad started getting you to do things like that?"

I purse my lips and don't reply. He's well aware that I was seven when it first happened, and he knows I don't like that it happened. At the time, I was just excited to earn some extra pocket money, but as I got older I realised that it was just one of my parents making me complicit in something illegal. Though I suppose that's still better than the other, who walked out on us not long before that.

I push the thoughts aside. I can't get distracted right now, either by my own past, or by what Zet's doing to the girl up the tree. I can convince him not to use little kids as lookouts another time.

The gate lets out a shrill squeak as Zet pulls it open, making my heart race and a new set of worries sink in about what's going to happen if we're caught now. Sometimes we can blag our way out of trouble, or more accurately, Zet can. I don't have the nerves or the ability to pull it off the way he can.

But this time is different. I don't think breaking into a burial ground in the middle of the night is something anyone can talk themselves out of.

"All right, come on," my best friend says, gesturing for me to follow him inside.

I grab the handle of the cart and pull it along behind me, hating every time the wheels bump over the ground. We're going to get into so much trouble if anyone stops us with it and asks to look through it. But entering any tomb is a one-time thing. Whatever we get tonight is going to be it, we have to make the most of it.

Zet uses his phone as a torch, flickering it over the entrances to the tombs. Some are above ground, while others are just a trap door covered by a flagstone. I don't need to ask to know which type we're looking for. Those who feel the need to be buried with their treasures always pick the underground option. They think it keeps them safer from thieves, when the reality is that it's just as easy for us to get to them if we're daring.

"This is the one," Zet says, coming to a stop in front of a trap door without a flagstone over it. There's a padlock around a chain on the door, but it's not going to stand in the way of Zet's bolt cutters any more than the one at the gate did.

The loud snap of the metal breaking is no easier to take than it was the first time, and I hate knowing how much attention it could draw. Zet doesn't seem to care, and pulls the trap door open, letting it fall back onto the ground with a soft thump.

"Ready?" he asks me.

"I guess," I murmur, pulling a headset with a torch out of my bag. I put it over my hat, making sure all of my blonde hair is tucked away and out of sight. One more way I can make it harder to identify me if everything does go wrong tonight.

I lower myself down through the trap door. My sleeve catches on the wooden frame, but I pull myself free easily enough.

A soft grunt escapes me as I reach the ground, landing easily from years of practice.

This might be my first time grave robbing, but the principles all remain the same.

I search around for a ladder, knowing there's going ro be one. There's no way they're bringing grave goods down here without one. It isn't hard to find, especially with Zet's torch above glinting off the gold inlay.

Whoever this tomb belongs to, it seems like they intend to try and take the ladder with them to the next life.

I flick on my own torch, illuminating the antechamber. The light flashes over the wall paintings, the vibrant paint feeling a bit like it's wasted on the dead. I know that's how things have always been, so that's what tombs look like, but it's still strange to see. No one I've ever known has been buried anywhere as lavish as this. For most of them, it's a basic wooden box if they're lucky, it definitely isn't a tomb with two rooms and an abundance of treasure.

"You out of the way?" Zet calls down.

"Yep. Sorry, just getting the ladder," I respond.

"No need."

I move out of the way just in time for Zet to land in the same spot I did.

"We can use the ladder for getting stuff out," he says, heading over to a pile of grave goods.

I look around properly, trying to take stock of what we're working with. It's going to take both of us and the ladder to get some of the stuff out, but it should be easy enough.

"Instructions are to start small. Jewels, gold, anything that can be broken down and sold easily."

"Yeah, I know the deal, Zet," I murmur. At least the occupant of the tomb isn't here yet. I'm already iffy enough about taking grave goods, but taking amulets and precious jewellery from his mummified body would be too much for me.

"You go left, I'll take the right."

I nod and head over to start checking through the items. A large mirror inlaid with jewels catches my attention and I pull out my pocket knife to remove a ruby from its setting. My hand slips as I try to make the cut, and my knife pricks me, as well as making the ruby crumble. "Argh."

"You okay?" Zet asks.

"Fake jewels and a cut," I respond, checking the slice in my glove. I'm going to need a new pair, which is going to cut into the proceeds from tonight. And that's if there are any real gems in here to even get us a haul in the first place.

"Just move on," he says.

I roll my eyes. This might be my first tomb, but it's not as if this is my first job, I know what I'm doing and the best way to do it.

I abandon the mirror and move through the other items in the room. There are several collars inlaid with precious and semi-precious stones that will be worth something even as they are, and I slip them into my bag, trying to ignore the tinge of guilt as I do.

I'm not even sure why I feel bad about this particular job. It's not like the dead guy is actually going to need this stuff in the afterlife. If it exists, and if it's really paradise, then why would he need to take things with him?

I push the thought aside. Now isn't the time to consider the afterlife, especially since by virtue of my life choices, I'm not going to be able to get there anyway. I carry on with my task, adding a few real jewels to my bag.

The torch flashes against the wall, illuminating a distinctive drawing of Ma'at in her red dress with wings outstretched and a feather perched on her head. The way the light falls on her makes it feel as if she's watching my every move and considering what I'm doing.

I pause for a moment and stare at her, trying to dismiss the feeling as part of my imagination. There's no way Ma'at has decided to watch a lowly thief from the wall of an obscure tomb in London. She'll have much bigger things to focus her attention on that aren't my misdemeanour.

"You ready to take things out?" Zet asks.

"Yeah." I pull my gaze away, veiling Ma'at in darkness. There's a part of me that can still feel her eyes on me.

"We'll go drop this stuff in the cart and then go down into the other room," Zet says.

"Do we have time for that?"

He shrugs. "Epi hasn't used the signal, we're fine."

I nod, not really wanting to spend more time down here than we need to, but realising that we have to make the most of it while we're already in the tomb. Which means getting rid of what we're already carrying and coming back for more.

# Chapter 4

A lot of clanking and crashing comes from the other side of the tomb where Zet is searching through the grave goods that are closer to where the body will actually be buried. From his curses, I don't think he's finding anything of particular interest.

It's not much better on this side of the room, but I can see that without rooting around in it. Years of doing this have honed my skills of spotting good stuff, I just don't tell anyone about it so they don't make me go on the really big jobs.

"All right, I think we should call it a night," Zet says, his frustration clear in his voice. He kicks at something on the floor, sending it skittering across the ground. "This could have gone better."

"I'm sorry." I'm frustrated as well, but a small part of me thinks that it makes sense. We're at a badly guarded burial ground not run by the Temple of Anubis. No one with any real wealth or power is going to be buried here. The chances are high that all of the graves around here are like this. Full of fake wealth and things that only look like they belong to someone of means. Though there's no doubt that the owner of this tomb is much better off than either me or Zet.

"Let's just get out of here, maybe we'll get something good on the way home," he says.

"We can't break in anywhere without casing it first," I remind him, mostly because I don't want to rather than anything else. Thankfully, I think the risk will be too much for Zet too.

"Yeah, you're right, especially when we already have stuff with us," he responds. "We'll just have to go out tomorrow night too to make up for it."

I grimace, but he doesn't see in the darkness. For which I'm glad. It's been a long time since

I've felt comfortable telling him how I feel about what we do. Especially when I don't really feel like I have a choice to do it. He doesn't talk about how he feels either, but I can see in his eyes how much he enjoys it.

He grabs his bag from where he left it on the coffin dais and swings it over his shoulder. I go to get my own, but pause when the light illuminates another wall painting.

Even though I know I shouldn't linger any longer, I stop to look at it properly. The golden scales dominate the scene, with a heart on one side and Ma'at's sacred feather on the other. The main test for entering the afterlife. There are supposed to be others, but they're irrelevant if you can't pass this one.

My gaze drifts to the right, where Ammit sits beyond the scales. Her open jaw is painted vividly with the deep green of the crocodile scales and the pearly white teeth, ready to devour the heart of any unworthy soul who ends up in the Hall of Judgement with a heart heavier than a feather.

I don't know enough hieroglyphs to be able to tell exactly what's going on, but I recognise the sign for a thief and my stomach sinks. If I believe what the priests say, then this is what the future holds for me.

"What are you looking at?" Zet asks.

"Nothing," I lie, pulling my attention away.

But he's too fast, moving to illuminate the wall himself. "The weighing of the heart?"

"I said it's nothing." I turn around and head towards the exit of the tomb. As much as I don't want to get caught in Ammit's powerful jaws, I also don't want to be caught in *this* life. Without the imminence of death hanging over me, that's far more important.

"I don't know why you let it bother you."

"Doesn't it bother *you*?" I respond as I throw my bag out of the tomb and hoist myself back up through the trap door.

Zet hands me his bag and I put both of them in the cart, glad we're not going to have to carry them the whole way. They're loud with the metal clanking together, and they're going to get heavy after not very long.

"I can't say I've really thought about it," he says once he's joined me.

"Our souls are damned for what we do," I point out.

He shrugs. "The gods aren't real, Rera. What do you care?"

"How can they not be real? The priests have magic."

"The priests *say* they have magic," he corrects me.

I chew on my lip, not entirely sure if I believe him or not. I suppose it's immaterial. Even if I believe in the gods, it's not like I have a choice in what I'm currently doing. If I don't steal, then I can't keep a roof over my head, or keep Meri in school. We could end up in the system, and as soon as I turn eighteen, there'll be no chance of me staying with Meri.

Tears sting at the corners of my eyes just thinking about it, but I blink them away.

We make our way to the exit of the burial grounds in awkward silence. I hate it when things become like this between us, but it happens almost every time we talk about the gods. I understand where he's coming from in a lot of ways. The gods haven't exactly been kind to either of us, and that's not really the kind of higher power that I want to have above us.

But it still leaves me with a lot of questions about how the world works if they *don't* exist.

Everyone has heard about the magic the priests possess. Whether it's the Ma'at Blessed's ability to tell when people are lying to them, or the Heka Blessed's ability to heal, the way the magic of the gods touches the world is supposedly undisputed. Though not to Zet from what he says.

The gate creaks loudly as he opens it, putting me right back on edge. This is going to be the worst time for us to get caught. We're coming out of the burial grounds and we have everything we've stolen on us. There won't be any way of us getting away with it.

Not that it's really an option anyway when there are priests who can tell when we're lying questioning us. The existence of those gifted with magic from the goddess of truth and justice makes it that much harder to get away with anything.

I push the thoughts to the side. I can spiral about what we do once I'm safely tucked in my own bed and out of the woods in terms of responsibility. There's always a chance it'll be traced back to us if someone talks, but unless that happens, we should be okay.

Zet shuts the gate behind us and puts the

padlock back in place despite the fact it's clearly cut. He lets out a low whistle, and a rustle from the trees announces Epi's return.

Even though I know what's happening, I still find myself tensing as the girl approaches. I really don't have the nerves to be breaking the law.

"Did you see anyone?" Zet asks.

She shakes her head. "Not even the guard."

"Good." He pulls out another couple of coins and gives them to her.

She runs off between two of the houses without looking back at us even for a second.

"You gave her double," I say to Zet, unable to hide my surprise.

He shrugs. "If we want her to keep her mouth shut, we have to pay her." Something about the way he says the words makes me not believe him. The extra money has nothing to do with Epi staying quiet and has everything to do with how he feels about what it was like for us to be the kids made to be lookouts.

I lift my hand to put it on his arm but think better of it. This isn't something he likes to talk about with me, so I shouldn't act like I can tell anything about it. We'll just go on pretending that his heart is hardened to the life we live, and the life we had as kids, and never speak about the truth of it.

That's just the way it has to be if we want to survive, and neither of us wants to mess with our chances of that.

# Chapter 5

The sky is already starting to grow lighter as we finally get back into our district of the city. I wish we had access to a car to make the journey a bit quicker, but neither of us can afford the expense, and it's not like we can use public transport when we have a cart full of stolen grave goods with us. Some of which are likely engraved with the deceased's name.

Another bolt of guilt passes through me as I think about it. I'm not sure why this type of theft sits with me more uneasily than others. Or maybe I just feel like it's worse right now because it's the job we've done tonight. If we'd been tasked to break and enter or to steal from one of the temples, I'd probably feel just as bad. This is just the thing I'm in the middle of.

And the one I could get caught in the act of doing.

The cart trundles along behind us, making a little bit too much noise for my liking, but no one seems to be paying us any attention. They've probably dismissed it as a car passing by or something like that.

"Rera!" Zet hisses, reaching out and grabbing my arm to pull me into an alley. He tugs the cart in alongside us.

"What's going on?" I ask.

He nods towards the street.

Nervously, I peer out of the alley, spotting two uniformed priests of Sekhmet with the hieroglyph for the war goddess blazoned on their jackets. My throat feels like it's closing up as I watch them pass. One look in our direction and we're going to be in their hands. It won't take them long to figure out what we've been up to.

The only thing in our favour is that they don't have a sacred lioness beside either of them.

I swallow hard. "At least they're not Blessed," I murmur.

"Mmm. Could be worse," Zet responds.

My heart races. If they catch us right now, we're doomed. They'll take us back to their temple for processing, then hand us over to the Temple of Ma'at. Even half an hour of processing there will have us condemned. Once the priests of the justice goddess get involved, there's nothing anyone can do to get away with their crime.

Neither of us moves as the patrol passes by.

"If we don't have to worry about the gods, why worry about them?" I murmur under my breath once they're far enough away that we don't have to worry about them.

"Because even if they don't have magic, enough people believe they do that they're going to take their word for it when we're caught," Zet responds, clearly assuming that my question was directed at him. He pulls the cart out of the alley and sets off in the direction of the hideout.

"Yeah, I know." I look off in the direction the priests have disappeared in. "Their power exists because we give it to them."

"I don't plan on giving the gods or the

temples any power over me," Zet responds firmly. "They can have me when I'm dead."

"They're not going to want you," I point out. "You'll be eaten by Ammit for your thieving ways."

He shrugs. "*If* the gods are real, and it's a real if, I'll just omit the *I have not stolen* portion of the declarations."

"I don't think it's as easy as that."

"They let people who have been to war and killed legally omit the not killing part," he counters.

"Well, yes. But the key there is *legally*," I remind him. "None of what we're doing is legal, and the gods you'd be making the proclamations to would know that. And it wouldn't help when your heart was weighed against Ma'at's feather either. The heart doesn't lie." And mine has been feeling particularly heavy of late.

"Should I be worried about you?" Zet asks. "You've been questioning the gods a lot lately."

"No." But his question is a good reminder that I should keep my thoughts to myself. Not many people in our line of work will be happy to hear I've been thinking about this kind of thing, never mind that I've been voicing them out loud.

"Nothing good comes from worshipping the gods, Rera. Or from worrying about them."

A part of me wants to point out that nothing good comes from ignoring them either, but I don't think he's going to listen to me on that front. I know all of his arguments for why the gods aren't real, I've heard them all countless times, and yet something about it all doesn't sit right with me. I wasn't brought up to be religious, and I don't remember my father ever mentioning the gods to me at all, but something deep within me rebels against the idea that the gods and the temples are all a figment of our imaginations and made to keep us all in line. There has to be more to it.

Though I suspect I won't find out the truth of the matter until I'm standing in the Hall of Judgement and Ammit is about to condemn my soul for not living an honest life. It won't even be entirely unfair of her to do that considering the life I've been living.

The wheel of the cart catches on a cobblestone, and the contents clank together louder than I'm comfortable with.

Zet tugs on the handle, but it seems well and truly stuck. His features twist in the lamplight, revealing that he's not as oblivious to the fear within me as I am.

"Just calm down," I tell him, trying to ignore my own racing heart. If we're unlucky, this is when someone is going to discover us, and then I don't even think that Zet's smooth-talking will be enough for them to leave us alone.

I crouch down beside the cart and fiddle with the wheel until it pulls free of the cobblestone.

Zet lets out a sigh of relief as he pulls it forward. "All right, good to go."

"You're welcome," I mutter, getting to my feet and wiping my hands on my clothes. They're black anyway, so a little bit of dirt isn't going to make a huge amount of difference.

"We should get back to HQ," he says.

I raise an eyebrow. "Isn't that what we've been doing?"

"We should get back faster."

I nod, not about to argue with him there. The patrol we already saw is far from the only one out tonight, and the longer we're out here, the more likely it is that we'll encounter another one. And there's always a chance that they'll have a Blessed priest with them. I'm not entirely sure what magic they allegedly possess, but even without that, the lion they'll have with them is enough.

I need to find a new line of work, because clearly, I don't have the nerves to be able to keep thieving. There's a certain amount of relief that comes with the realisation, though it's quickly followed by dread. I don't know *how* I'm going to find another job, and the options are limited to me without finishing school.

But hopefully, I'll be able to find a way free of the mess I've already made of my life.

# Chapter 6

My whole body is aching by the time we get
back to HQ and I'm ready to collapse into my
bed and ignore the world for the next few hours.
But that's not possible. First, we need to unload
everything we've got, then I can deal with my
own needs. At least that's going to mean that I'll
no longer have stolen goods in my possession,
just money from procuring them.

"Get the door for me, will you?" Zet asks.

I hurry forward and pull up the horizontal
door. It clacks loudly as it moves above my head,
and I wince at the thought of it alerting
someone that we're up to no good. Then again,
the neighbours on this street don't care. Most of
them are *also* up to no good, so it's not like

they're going to bring any of the patrolling priests to our door.

I'm still relieved when Zet rolls the cart inside and lets me pull down the shutter behind him, taking us out of sight of anyone on the street and one step closer to being free of tonight's job. It won't put us completely in the clear, but it will move us one step closer.

"Let's get this over with," he says. "I'm starving."

"Mmm. And I need to get home to make sure Meri gets off to school okay." At this rate, I should be home in time for her to be getting up.

"She's thirteen, she's capable of getting to school on her own."

"Wouldn't you have skipped school when you were thirteen if you could?" I ask him.

"We did," he reminds me. "Many, many, times."

"And look where that got us," I mutter.

"Is it really so bad?" he asks. "We've got free-dom, adventure, and we see things we'd never get a chance to otherwise."

"Are you saying that the people we steal from deserve to have things taken?" I can't help the disbelief that comes through my voice.

Zet looks around to make sure no one else is in this part of the hideout and then tugs me closer to him. "You can't talk like that here."

"And when *can* I talk like that? In front of the little sister I'm supposed to provide for because our dad is off doing whatever it is he's doing? Or when we're in the middle of a job where I'm trying to earn enough money so that we can eat this week?"

"Why do this if you hate it so much?" he snaps.

"Because I have to, Zet," I remind him. "No one else is going to employ me, and I need to protect Meri."

He rolls his eyes. "Just get your dad to do it if you're worrying about her so much."

"I don't even know where he is." Anger rises within me, though it's hard to figure out if it's directed at Zet or my dad. Or if it's aimed at myself. There's really no way for me to tell other than to know that I *am* angry.

"Let's just get our money and go sleep," my best friend says. "We can deal with the rest of this later."

"Mmm." I know we're not going to. He doesn't want a conversation with me about what our jobs entail and why they're bad. That would involve both of us facing some difficult truths.

He takes my response at face value and pulls the cart through to the other room. There are more people in here, though they're thankfully talking amongst themselves and probably didn't hear any of what we were talking about. At least, that's my hope. It's bad enough having Zet know how unhappy I am about my position in the thieving crew, it would be a lot worse if any of the others found out.

And if it got back to my dad. I don't know what he'd do if he found out, but I don't imagine it'll be good.

I recognise several teams who must have also been out on jobs tonight, but Geo and Akar are nowhere to be seen. I suppose they could have already been, but that seems unlikely when they'll have had a better haul than we have.

Rimes dismisses the team he's talking to and calls the next one to the front of the room, going through the process of surveying what they've stolen and deciding what it's worth.

My skin crawls like it does every time I see the tall bald man. There's something about him that sets me on edge, like I can tell that he's not a safe person to be around just by looking at him.

All of my aches seem to be magnified by ten while we wait to be seen by him. Several of the other teams take their turns showing him their takings, and he gives most of them money in return. I wish we didn't have to deal with this part, but the alternative is trying to fence the stuff we stole ourselves, and that's dangerous in itself. People will wonder where a ragged-looking seventeen-year-old got a load of rubies. It's better to let someone else deal with that part.

We're gestured forward, and Zet drags the cart to a stop in front of Rimes.

"We raided a tomb in the Tower Hamlets burial grounds," Zet says, pushing forward the cart.

One of Rimes' goons comes forward and searches through everything we've got while I stand nervously to the side. If they don't think what we've got is worth anything then we're going to be in trouble. Rent's due next week and if I don't get enough together, our landlord is going to kick us out.

The goon heads back to Rimes and says something in his ear.

"Three hundred debens," Rimes says decisively.

"Each?" Zet asks hopefully, but I know what's coming next. I've never known the boss to be as generous as that, and our haul isn't particularly great quality. If I'm honest, I'm surprised he's giving us that much.

"Total." He gestures for one of his helpers, who produces the bank notes, handing them over to Zet.

"The stuff we got for you is worth at least ten times that," Zet protests.

He's exaggerating a bit, but it's definitely worth more than we're being paid. Rimes will make a tidy profit on his end by giving us so little. Which is how he stays in charge. Everyone else does the dirty work and he profits from it.

Rimes looks down at us with a dismissive expression on his face. "Three hundred is generous."

"It's not..." Zet starts to protest.

I grimace, wishing my best friend would just accept what we've got and not cause any waves. Attracting the attention of a man like Rimes is never wise.

"You use my equipment, you use my intel,

and you use my protection," Rimes says, a note of anger in his voice. "If you want none of that, then I can take back the money, and keep tonight's take as your severance fee."

"Three hundred is fine," I say firmly. As much as I wish we weren't under Rimes' control, I don't want to lose the money we've got.

"Don't you know who Rera's..." Zet starts.

"Zet, no," I hiss at my best friend.

He gives me an odd look. "All right, fine. Three hundred debens."

Rimes waves us away, the look on his face saying he's not happy with us, and that next time we bring him stuff, he's going to give us an even worse price for it.

"Why do you have to make him angry?" I mutter to Zet, once we're back out on the street and safely out of earshot of anyone in the den. I feel better now we don't have any of the tomb's contents on us, and we've dropped our tools back off in the process too. Now we're just two teenagers out for a pre-dawn walk, which is suspicious but not illegal.

"He isn't giving us what our work is worth," he counters.

"He doesn't pay anyone what the stuff they

bring is worth," I remind him. "We're not special."

"But you are. If you just told him who your dad was..."

"What? He'd suddenly start treating us better?" I snap. "It's more likely to make things worse."

"I doubt that."

I raise an eyebrow. "I don't. You know what it's like with rival teams and people wanting to outdo the others. If he knows who my dad is, then it'll make me a pawn in a much more dangerous game."

Zet finally nods in acknowledgement. "All right, fine. I'll keep quiet about it."

"Thank you."

"But I still think you should use it to your advantage more."

"I'm really not going to," I respond.

"You could climb through the ranks faster. Get us better, less dangerous jobs."

"Mmm." I don't add that I don't *want* to rise through the ranks. I'm not trying to be a daring thief, I'm just trying to survive.

"Just think about it, Rera, all right? If you're higher up, we'll have more money, and you won't have to struggle as much with Meri."

"If we're higher up, then there's also more chance of us getting caught. More people will know who we are, and they might hand us over for a more lenient sentence from the Temple of Ma'at. It won't help Meri if I'm inside the temple and not able to get out."

He sighs. "You've made up your mind without actually thinking it through."

"And you haven't?" I snap. "This isn't some glorious life of stealing from the rich and giving to the poor, Zet. What we do hurts people."

He scoffs. "Hardly. We're not doing anything to put anyone in harm's way."

"And what about the guy we stole from tonight?" I can't help the anger rising within me. He just doesn't seem to get it.

"Eurgh, are you seriously still on with that?"

"It was a few hours ago, we literally just handed over his grave goods in exchange for a few hundred debens. So yeah, I'm still on that."

"I don't know why you're suddenly so obsessed with the gods and the afterlife. You never used to care about angering them."

I frown, wondering if he's right and where

this is all coming from. We learned about the gods in school, but I've never seen much of a reason to go to any of the temples. So why am I suddenly feeling like this?

"I'm just tired," I murmur. It's only partially a lie, but it's better than telling him that I have no idea where any of this is coming from. I don't think that's going to be the explanation he wants right now.

He deflates in front of me, seeming relieved that I've not given him an actual argument. If I'm honest with myself, I am too. I don't want to be in a fight with him, especially not over something as ridiculous as the gods and whether or not they exist. Even if they do, they're not affecting my life and it's better if I just leave it that way.

"Let's just go home and I'll see you tomorrow," I say.

"All right." He shoves his hand into his pocket and counts out the notes. "Here you go."

"Thanks." I shove it in my pocket, trying not to think about how little it actually is and how far it has to go. There's a part of me that wants to be reckless and go find a bakery to buy something fun to eat, especially with the rumbling in my stomach, but I know that's not the smartest idea. I could buy a lot more with it at the supermarket, and save the rest for rent.

"See you tomorrow, Rera."

"You too." I wave goodbye to him and set off home, my hands in my pockets and my head bowed. I hate this part. It feels like I'm walking through London with the shame of my crime written all over me, and that people will be able to tell what it is just by looking at me. I know that isn't logical, but I can't help it.

The sooner I can figure out how to break free of this life, the better. I just wish I knew where to start.

# Chapter 7

A pounding breaks through my sleep and I roll over, groaning as I do. It's definitely not been long enough since I got into bed for me to be awake.

"All right, I'm coming!" I call loudly, though there's a chance Zet can't hear me through the walls. "You could just let yourself in," I mutter, assuming it's Zet on the other side of the door.

My hair is a mess, and my sleep shirt barely covers me, but it's not like he hasn't seen me this way before, and if he's waking me up so early, then he'll know that I'll have been in bed.

The whole flat is cold, and I wish I'd grabbed myself a jumper before leaving my bedroom, but it's too late for that.

There's another bang on the front door.

"Seriously, you need to chill out, Zet. Do you have any idea how little sleep I've had?" I ask as I pull the door open, only to stop in my tracks when I see Geo on the other side. "You're not Zet."

His eyes are wide and bloodshot, and he's shaking. He runs a hand through his red hair, only making him seem more on edge.

"Are you okay?" Concern fills me as I look at my friend.

He shakes his head. "Can I come in?"

"Sure. I don't have much I can offer you..." Maybe that isn't what I should be worrying about right now, but I still want to be a good hostess.

"Don't need it." He enters the room, and sits down on the threadbare sofa, looking a little bit better.

I shut the door and bolt it, fearing whatever it is that's got him so worked up. "What's going on?"

"Akar got caught."

Something drops in the pit of my stomach. "What?"

"He got caught." He takes a shaky breath. "I

didn't know where to go. I couldn't go to my flat, he might have told them where I live already. And I couldn't go to Akar's place, they're going to have people there already. I tried Zet, but he wasn't answering."

"He's not?" Worry worms its way through me. What if he's done something dumb and gotten himself caught? He wasn't happy with what Rimes gave us, so it's not impossible that he'd go do another job without me.

"Haven't you talked to him today?"

"I've been asleep since I got back." It's probably best I don't mention my worries, or that the two of us argued last night. I like Geo, and I don't think he's going to start talking about me to other people, but I can't take the risk, especially not when there's so much at stake.

"Oh. Right." He rubs a hand over his face. "I don't know what to do right now."

"We'll figure it out," I promise. "I think I have some old coffee grounds, I can make you a cup." I head to the cupboard and pull it out.

"You don't have to do that."

I shrug. "I don't drink it, I don't even know why we have it." I flick on the kettle and dump some of the brown powder into the mug.

"Thanks, Rera."

"No problem. I know you'd do the same for me."

"I can stay here today, right?" The pleading look in his eyes is hard to ignore.

"Yeah, sure." It seems unlikely that the priests will track Geo here, and that's even if Akar has said anything. I finish making Geo's coffee and put it down in front of him.

He offers me a weak smile.

"I'm just going to go grab a jumper," I say, gesturing in the direction of my room. Though I also intend on messaging Zet, because a part of me is worrying a lot about the fact he didn't answer Geo's knocking. He's not *that* heavy of a sleeper.

I pull on some leggings as well as a jumper, not wanting to be quite so exposed with someone else in the flat. I type out a quick message to Zet, telling him to check in and that Akar has been arrested so he's not blindsided by it when he turns up.

I head back out to see Geo wrapped up and looking much younger than eighteen, his hands around his mug of bad coffee, and a strained expression on his face.

"It's going to be okay," I assure him, sitting down at the kitchen table and wishing I had something to offer him to eat, but I was too tired to go and get anything from the store before coming home to collapse. My rumbling stomach is also telling me how much of a mistake that is. I haven't had anything to eat since Akar brought us the wraps last night.

"You don't know that," Geo protests.

"Do they have anything on him?" I ask.

He shakes his head. "I managed to hide with our bags before they arrested him."

"Okay, so he doesn't have anything to tie him to any robberies," I say. "So long as he doesn't *tell* them anything, they can't catch him out. They can only tell we're lying if we tell them a lie."

Geo lets out a sigh of relief. "I forgot about that."

"Akar won't have," I promise, though I'm not entirely sure if that's true. "It's going to be all he can think about right now." At least, that's all I'm going to be able to think about if I end up in Ma'at's Temple. It's not that it's impossible to conceal the truth, it's just impossible to lie, and those are two very different things.

"You're right."

I press the button on my phone to check if Zet's responded, but there's nothing. A horrible feeling settles within me. What if he's also been caught?

I take a deep breath. I shouldn't borrow trouble that doesn't exist yet. If Zet has been caught, he'll be fine. He's got the charm to be able to use it to his advantage.

"This is all my fault," Geo murmurs, pushing his empty cup away and leaning his head against his knees.

"It's not your fault," I assure him quickly. "It could happen to any of us. It's one of the dangers of the job."

"Yeah, but Akar doesn't need to do this like we do," he counters. "His folks have got their shop, and he's going to go work there after he's finished with school. I just convinced him it would be fun and that he'd be able to earn a little extra cash."

I grimace, trying not to judge him too badly for that. It's kind of how Zet and I started with the whole situation, so I can't really pretend that I don't understand. It just transitioned into something we both needed to do afterwards.

"His parents don't even know," he says. "They're going to find out. If they charge him, then they're going to find out."

"Let's hope that doesn't happen then," I respond. "And that one of us can be there when he gets out so he doesn't need to call them."

"I don't think I can do that. What if they can tell we worked together?" The pained expression on his face twists at my insides.

"I'll go."

"What? No, you can't put yourself in danger."

I shrug. "I don't know anything about what the two of you did last night. They'll probably just think I'm his girlfriend or something."

Geo snorts. "Yeah, 'cause Zet is going to *love* that," he mumbles.

"What? Why would Zet care what I say to the Temple of Ma'at about Akar?"

He raises an eyebrow. "You have no idea, do you?"

"Clearly not," I mutter. I'm about to ask him more when a key turns in the lock and someone tries to open the door.

"Eurgh, Rera, you left the bolt on again," Zet's voice comes through.

I let out a sigh of relief, followed by frustration that he couldn't even message me to tell me he was okay.

"Let me in."

"I'm coming," I call back, heading over to the door and pushing it shut properly so I can undo the bolt. I pull it open to find my friend on the other side.

He looks me up and down, surprise on his face. "You're awake."

"You'd know that if you looked at your phone once in a while," I mutter.

"What?" He pulls it out. "Argh, it died. I forgot to put it on charge when I got in. But I brought you breakfast to make up for last night." He holds up a bag.

"You have nothing to make up for, we were both just tired." It's a lie, but I don't want to get into our differences in opinion again.

I let him inside. He stops in his tracks when he spots Geo on the sofa.

"You're not alone," he says, a weird emotion in his voice that I can't tell what it is. He looks between me and Geo as if trying to make out what's going on.

"You'd know that if you checked your phone

too," I tell him. "There's a charger on the counter."

He nods and goes over to plug it in. "So, what will I find out when my phone is on?"

"Akar got arrested last night," I say.

"And you came *here*?" he asks Geo, a hint of anger in his voice.

"I didn't know where else to go," our friend responds.

"You're welcome here anytime," I say. "Just like you are," I point out to my best friend.

He mumbles something I don't catch under his breath, but I ignore him. It's probably better that way.

"You said something about breakfast?" I ask. I might not actually need him to make up for what happened last night, but I'm hungry and there's no food in the flat.

He hands me the bag and I smile at him, glad when I discover enough inside for all of us to share. I get out the chopping board and bread knife and start cutting the freshly baked bread. Zet shouldn't have wasted the money he did on something as fancy as this, but I appreciate it all the same.

"I have a bit of jam in the cover by your head if you want it," I say to Zet.

He nods and gets it out, along with a knife. It's only now Geo is here that I start wondering if it's strange that Zet knows his way around my kitchen like this. Especially because it's not *just* the kitchen he knows his way around, but the whole flat.

I keep that thought to myself and focus on eating, taking it as slow as I can so I don't give myself indigestion, even though I feel hungry enough to eat the whole loaf by myself.

Geo tentatively takes a bite, while Zet looks at him oddly.

The whole room is tense, and I'm glad that Meri is at school and not having to deal with all of this weirdness.

None of us say anything until Geo's phone lights up. He picks it up, a nervous expression on his face. "What do I do? I don't know the number."

"Answer it," I respond. "It could be Akar."

He nods and presses the answer button, putting it to his ear. "Hello? Yes...okay...someone will be there." He puts down the phone and lets out a sigh of relief.

"He's being released?" I guess.

"Yeah. In an hour."

"All right, that gives me enough time to get there," I say. "You two will be all right here, won't you?"

"You're not going to the Temple of Ma'at," Zet says firmly.

"Yes, I am," I respond. "Akar needs someone there so his parents don't find out. Geo can't go, so I'm going."

"But..."

"This isn't a discussion, Zet," I say firmly. "I'm going." I turn on my heels and head to my bedroom to get dressed. I don't particularly want to go to the Temple of Ma'at, but I also don't want to leave my friend in the lurch.

And that's enough to get me out of the door and to the last place I want to be.

## Chapter 8

The closer I get to Ma'at's Temple, the more I start thinking that this is a bad idea. I may not have had anything to do with Geo and Akar's job last night, but I was still up to no good, and if the right person asks me the right question while I'm inside, then I could end up in just as much trouble as Akar.

Probably more. Grave robbing is seen as a particularly bad crime.

I push the thoughts aside. I promised Geo that I'd help, and Akar doesn't deserve to be left inside.

There's a vast difference between where I live and Temple Street. The Thames flows behind the temples, and I can hear shouts from the river, but it's not just that. Everything is clean here, and the buildings are huge, with each of them dedicated to one of the major gods. This isn't the only part of London that's taken over by temples, they're everywhere, especially those dedicated to the gods who influence daily life, but this is where most of the central temples are and it shows.

A dozen cats hang by a side door into the Temple of Bastet, while a priestess seems to feed them from a basket. They meow loudly, but they don't pay any attention to anyone else.

I carry on up the street, passing the temples of Thoth, Taweret, and Seth, each of them seeming more grand than the last.

The sprawling Temple of Anubis makes me pause with the two grand statues of the god on either side of the entrance. It feels like he's judging me for what I did last night, taking from the dead is something the god of mummification likely frowns upon.

The gates open and I tense as a dark-haired priestess with a jackal by her side leaves, talking away to the tall man on her left. Despite the fact none of her powers will revolve around catching criminals, I still find myself on edge in the presence of one of the gods' Blessed. If what the priesthood says is true, this woman has magic gifted to her by Anubis himself.

I pull my attention away and hurry down the street with my head bowed, ignoring the other temples as much as possible in case I see a Blessed whose job it actually is to catch me. I do my best to avoid those gifted by the gods, it's better for surviving.

I finally reach the Temple of Ma'at and realise that all of my avoidance of Blessed is about to come to an end. Inside there are going to be dozens of priests and priestesses who are able to tell when I lie to them, which means I need to use all of the wits available to me to make sure they don't catch me doing just that. I take a deep breath.

Imposing statues of the goddess flank the entrance to the temple, looking out and judging the people passing by. It's both more and less intimidating than I expected it to be. I slowly make my way up the steps, passing beneath them and feeling a little better now that I'm inside.

Signposts make it clear where I'm supposed to go, and I make my way through the corridors, avoiding eye contact with everyone here. I feel underdressed compared to the workers at the temple. They all feel so pristinely put together that it's kind of intimidating, but I know I shouldn't let it get to me. They have a good place to live, food, and employment stability. Those things are going to make them more poised than I am.

I finally get to the reception to pick up people being released by the temple, and I head over to the bored-looking scribe behind the desk.

I try to find any indication that he might be Blessed, but unfortunately, the Ma'at Blessed don't come with a handy animal companion to announce that they've been chosen by the gods. Which raises a lot of questions of how they even find out. Can they just randomly tell when people are lying and that's how they discover that Ma'at has chosen them?

I suppose it's one of the many things that's going to remain a complete mystery to me. It's not like I'm ever going to know a Blessed Priest of Ma'at to ask them.

"Can I help?" the scribe asks, barely looking up from his paperwork.

"Hi, I'm here to pick someone up," I say, my voice shaking with nerves.

"Name?"

"Akar," I respond. "He's been waiting for about twenty minutes."

The scribe looks up at me, an unimpressed expression on his face. "Your name."

"Oh, Rera. No, sorry, Aurera. You probably want my full name, right?"

"Do I look like I care?" the scribe responds. "Who are you? Akar's sister?"

"No."

"Girlfriend?"

"We're family." I don't want to prolong the conversation or try to explain how I actually know him, so it's better to go for something that won't be seen as me lying. We're not related, but we're a family of sorts, which should be enough to stop this man from knowing if I'm lying or not. If he can even tell. There's no way of being certain which of the people working at the Temple of Ma'at have the ability and who doesn't. They probably do that on purpose so people don't lie to any of them.

"Wait over there." He waves towards some empty seats.

There are a couple of other people in the waiting room, but none of them pay me any attention as I head over to one of the chairs and sit down. I wring my hands together, trying not to worry too much about where I am. I shouldn't be here, and walking through the doors voluntarily isn't something anyone should be doing.

But I also can't let Akar come out and be alone. That's too much for any one person to deal with.

I look around, taking in the intricate wall paintings. The hieroglyphics mean nothing to me, but the images that go along with them tell me enough. The walls depict various priests of Ma'at doing their duty. The one opposite makes me swallow hard as I can see them questioning someone who seems to be branded a thief.

I know the people on the walls aren't real, and they're just generalised profiles of what the situation would look like, but I can't help considering how much the thief looks like Zet. It's only a matter of time before he ends up here to be questioned, just like Akar is now.

The woman opposite me is sobbing quietly, though there's no indication of why. It could be anything, though considering this is the office for people being released from custody, it can't be that bad.

A thud sounds and I look up in time to see Akar appear in the doorway. He looks tired, but that's to be expected. He heads over to the desk and they give him a bag of his possessions back.

I get to my feet and head over. "Akar."

He turns, surprise on his face. "Rera."

Not wanting to raise any suspicions in case anyone is watching us, I go to hug him.

He pats my back awkwardly, which makes sense. This is probably the most contact the two of us have ever shared.

"Come on, let's get out of here," I say.

He nods, pulling back but not questioning my appearance here, which is something at least.

I can sense Akar's nervousness as we make our way back through the temple. I want to ask him what happened while he was inside, but I don't want to be overheard by anyone.

It isn't until we're outside that I let out a sigh of relief. "Are you okay?" I ask him.

He nods, looking as relieved as I feel, or

even more so. "I'm fine. How come you're here?"

"Geo sent me. We thought it would be better if I came when I don't know anything about what went on last night."

"Oh, so Geo's okay?"

"He's fine," I assure him. "And your parents know nothing."

He nods. "I feel like an idiot. I don't think I ever thought about getting caught until last night."

I reach out and put what I hope is a comforting hand on his arm. "It'll be okay."

"Yeah." Indecision wars on his face. "Do you mind if I walk home alone? I know you came all this way to get me, but I really just want time to think."

"Sure." I flash him a reassuring smile. "Maybe let Geo know you're out and safe first though, he's at mine worrying."

"Of course."

"And if your parents ask, just say you spent the night hanging out with us at my place and fell asleep." I don't know what makes me offer up the excuse to him, but I can tell that he's worried about how they're going to react to him being arrested by the Temple of Ma'at.

"Thanks, Rera."

"Any time." I wave at him as he heads down the street.

I let him go, not entirely sure what to do with myself. I could head back to my flat, but once I get there, I'm going to have to deal with Geo and Zet. Though I suppose the former will probably go home now Akar is free and he's not in danger of being caught.

I turn around, my gaze drawn to the Temple of Ma'at and the statues outside it. They're not as imposing from this distance, and it almost looks as if Ma'at has an understanding expression on her face. I shake the thought free of my head. It's just a trick of the light making me think that.

A strange feeling settles within me as I look at the temple, like I know I'm going to end up here. It's not an outrageous possibility, most thieves end up having a brush with the Temple of Ma'at, it's only a matter of time before it's me.

But this feeling is different. It's almost as if

ending up here isn't going to be the end of my freedom, but the beginning.

Thank you for reading *All Chaos For Thieves*, I hope you enjoyed it. If you want to find out more about what happens when Rera does have her brush with the Temple of Ma'at (in a rather unexpected way!) in *No Justice For Thieves*, the first book in the *Scales Of Justice* series: https://books.authorlauragreenwood.co.uk/nojusticeforthieves

And if you want to meet some of the other important characters from the *Scales Of Justice* series (including Rera's love interest!) you can download *Legacy Of Wings* for free: https://books.authorlauragreenwood.co.uk/shan

## Author Note

Thank you for reading *All Chaos For Thieves*, I hope you enjoyed it.

This is probably your first taste of Rera - and it's mine too. She's never appeared as a side character in any of the other books. It's been a lot of fun getting to know her and the kind of person she is, especially when she's so enmeshed in the London underworld - which isn't the sort of character I normally write.

This prequel is also unusual in that Rera's love interest hasn't made an appearance yet. I did consider whether this was the right thing to do, but as Benipe was introduced in *Legacy Of Wings* (a side story set in my Egyptian Empire world) I thought it would be fine - and this is an important introduction into Rera, her motivations, and some of the important side characters around her for when her series starts to unfold.

As with the other books set in the Egyptian Empire series, the characters have been named after real people from Ancient Egypt, those we know about from wall paintings, tombs, and papyri. The difference with the names in *All Chaos For Thieves*, is that I either chose already short names, or I shortened them and didn't reveal the longer version - this is mostly just to keep up the feel of the world Rera is living in, and how different it is from the one Ani inhabits in *The Apprentice Of Anubis*.

If you're completely new to the world, then you may or may not have noticed a lot of nods to not just Egyptian mythology, but also to Ancient Egyptian life as it was - the characters' phones don't have cameras, the currency is named after bread, the belief in curses and magic. More will become clear as the series unfolds and Rera finds herself deeper into both the underworld of London and the more elite space of the temples.

For those of you who have been long-time readers of my *Apprentice of Anubis series*, you might have noticed the very brief (from a distance!) cameo of Ani, Nik, and Matia. This was mostly just for fun as it's unlikely Rera and Ani's paths will cross anytime soon.

If you can't wait for the first book in the series to find out more about the Temple of Ma'at, there is an Egyptian Empire side story, *Scales Of Honesty*, that follows Taia, a Blessed Priestess - and Taia will be a side character further into the series too!

If you want to keep up to date with new releases and other news, you can join my Facebook Reader Group or mailing list.

Stay safe & happy reading!

- Laura

## Get A Free Scales Of Justice Story

**A family legacy is a lot to live up to - especially for Nephthys' newest apprentice.**

Shan knows her parents expect a lot from her, especially when it comes to which of the Egyptian gods she'll serve after the Day of Choosing.

Despite knowing what she wants, Shan finds herself questioning her place in the temple, and whether Nephthys has chosen to bless her with magic for the right reasons.

But with her twin brother, and his best friend,

by her side encouraging her, can she finally claim the place that's rightfully hers?

-

*Legacy Of Wings* is a standalone companion story to *The Apprentice Of Anubis* & Scales *Of Justice* series, an urban fantasy set in an alternative version of London where the Egyptian Empire never fell. Legacy Of Wings can be read as a standalone and includes a brother's best friend/friends to lovers m/f romance.

You can download Legacy Of Wings for free here: https://books.authorlauragreenwood.co.uk/shan

# Also by Laura Greenwood

You can find out more about each of my series on my website.


- Obscure Academy: a paranormal romance series set at a university-age academy for mixed supernaturals. Each book follows a different couple.
- The Apprentice Of Anubis: an urban fantasy series set in an alternative world where the Ancient Egyptian Empire never fell. It follows a new apprentice to the temple of Anubis as she learns about her new role.
- Forgotten Gods: a paranormal adventure romance series inspired by Egyptian mythology. Each book follows a different Ancient Egyptian goddess.
- Amethyst's Wand Shop Mysteries (with Arizona Tape): an urban fantasy murder mystery series following a witch who teams up with a detective to solve murders. Each book includes a different murder.

- Grimm Academy: a fantasy fairy tale academy series. Each book follows a different fairy tale heroine.
- Jinx Paranormal Dating Agency: a paranormal romance series based on worldwide mythology where paranormals and deities take part in events organised by the Jinx Dating Agency. Each book follows a different couple.
- Purple Oak Oasis (with Arizona Tape): a cozy fantasy romance series with unusual magic. Each book follows a different couple.
- House Of Blood And Roses: a vampire fantasy romance series following a heroine who discovers she's a vampire noble and has to navigate a world full of politics, betrayal, and blood lust.
- Scales Of Justice: an urban fantasy following a thief who accidentally becomes the newest apprentice of the goddess of truth.
- Speed Dating With The Denizens Of The Underworld (shared world): a paranormal romance shared world based on mythology from around the world. Each book follows a different couple.

- Blackthorn Academy For Supernaturals
  (shared world): a paranormal monster
  romance shared world based at
  Blackthorn Academy. Each book follows
  a different couple.

You can find a complete list of all my books on my website:

https://books.authorlauragreenwood.co.uk/book-list

Signed Paperback & Merchandise:

You can find signed paperbacks, hardcovers, and merchandise based on my series (including stickers, magnets, face masks, and more!) via my website:

https://books.authorlauragreenwood.co.uk/shop

# About Laura Greenwood

Laura is a USA Today Bestselling Author of paranormal romance, urban fantasy, and fantasy romance. When she's not writing, she drinks a lot of tea, tries to resist French macarons, and works towards a diploma in Egyptology. She lives in the UK, where most of her books are set. Laura specialises in quick reads, with healthy relationships and consent-positive moments regardless of if she's writing light-hearted romance, mythology-heavy urban fantasy, or anything in between.

Follow Laura Greenwood

- Website: www.authorlaura-greenwood.co.uk
- Mailing List: https://books.authorlauragreenwood.co.uk/newsletter
- Facebook Group: http://facebook.com/groups/theparanormalcouncil

- Facebook Page: http://facebook.com/authorlauragreenwood
- Bookbub: https://www.bookbub.com/authors/laura-greenwood